THIS NOTEBOOK BELONGS TO

Made in the USA
Monee, IL
29 March 2021

64286517R00056